PICTURES DON'T LIE

PICTURES DON'T LIE

by Katherine MacLEAN

The man from the *News* asked, "What do you think of the aliens, Mister Nathen? Are they friendly? Do they look human?"

"Very human," said the thin young man.

Outside, rain sleeted across the big windows with a steady faint drumming, blurring and dimming the view of the airfield where *they* would arrive. On the concrete runways, the puddles were pockmarked with rain, and the grass growing untouched between the runways of the unused field glistened wetly, bending before gusts of wind.

Back at a respectful distance from where the huge spaceship would land were the gray shapes of trucks, where TV camera crews huddled inside their mobile units, waiting. Farther back in the deserted sandy landscape, behind distant sandy hills, artillery was ringed in a great circle, and in the distance across the horizon, bombers stood ready at airfields, guarding the world against possible treachery from the first alien ship ever to land from space.

"Do you know anything about their home planet?" asked the man from *Herald*.

The *Times* man stood with the others, listening absently, thinking of questions, but reserving them. Joseph R. Nathen, the thin young man with the straight black hair and the tired lines on his face, was being treated with respect by his interviewers. He was obviously on edge, and they did not want to harry him with too many questions to answer at once. They wanted to keep his good will. Tomorrow he would be one of the biggest celebrities ever to appear in headlines.

"No, nothing directly."

"Any ideas or deductions?" *Herald* persisted.

"Their world must be Earth-like to them," the weary-looking young man answered uncertainly. "The environment evolves the animal. But only in relative terms, of course." He looked at them with a quick glance and then looked away evasively, his lank black hair beginning to cling to his forehead with sweat. "That doesn't necessarily mean anything."

"Earth-like," muttered a reporter, writing it down as if he had noticed nothing more in the reply.

The *Times* man glanced at the *Herald*, wondering if he had noticed, and received a quick glance in exchange.

The *Herald* asked Nathen, "You think they are dangerous, then?"

It was the kind of question, assuming much, which usually broke reticence and brought forth quick facts—when it hit the mark. They all knew of the military precautions, although they were not supposed to know.

The question missed. Nathen glanced out the window vaguely. "No, I wouldn't say so."

"You think they are friendly, then?" said the *Herald*, equally positive on the opposite tack.

A fleeting smile touched Nathen's lips. "Those I know are."

There was no lead in this direction, and they had to get the basic facts of the story before the ship came. The *Times* asked, "What led up to your contacting them?"

Nathen answered after a hesitation. "Static. Radio static. The Army told you my job, didn't they?"

*

The Army had told them nothing at all. The officer who had conducted them in for the interview stood glowering watchfully, as if he objected by instinct to telling anything to the public.

Nathen glanced at him doubtfully. "My job is radio decoder for the Department of Military Intelligence. I use a directional pickup, tune in on foreign bands, record any scrambled or coded messages I hear, and build automatic decoders and descramblers for all the basic scramble patterns."

The officer cleared his throat, but said nothing.

The reporters smiled, noting that down.

Security regulations had changed since arms inspection had been legalized by the U.N. Complete information being the only public security against secret rearmament, spying and prying had come to seem a public service. Its aura had changed. It was good public relations to admit to it.

Nathen continued, "I started directing the pickup at stars in my spare time. There's radio noise from stars, you know. Just stuff that sounds like spatter static, and an occasional squawk. People have been listening to it for a long time, and researching, trying to work out why stellar radiation on those bands comes in such jagged bursts. It didn't seem natural."

He paused and smiled uncertainly, aware that the next thing he would say was the thing that would make him famous—an idea that had come to him while he listened—an idea as simple and as perfect as the one that came to Newton when he saw the apple fall.

"I decided it wasn't natural. I tried decoding it."

Hurriedly he tried to explain it away and make it seem obvious. "You see, there's an old intelligence trick, speeding up a message on a record until it sounds just like that, a short squawk of static, and then broadcasting it. Undergrounds use it. I'd heard that kind of screech before."

"You mean they broadcast at us in code?" asked the *News*.

"It's not exactly code. All you need to do is record it and slow it down. They're not broadcasting at us. If a star has planets, inhabited planets, and there is broadcasting between them, they would send it on a tight beam to save power." He looked for comprehension. "You know, like a spotlight. Theoretically, a tight beam can go on forever without losing power. But aiming would be difficult from planet to planet. You can't expect a beam to stay on target, over such distances, more than a few seconds at a time. So they'd naturally compress each message into a short half-second or one-second-length package and send it a few hundred times in one long blast to make sure it is picked up during the instant the beam swings across the target."

He was talking slowly and carefully, remembering that this explanation was for the newspapers. "When a stray beam swings through our section of space, there's a sharp peak in noise level from that direction. The beams are swinging to follow their own planets at home, and the distance between there and here exaggerates the speed of swing tremendously, so we wouldn't pick up more than a bip as it passes."

"How do you account for the number of squawks coming in?" the *Times* asked. "Do stellar systems rotate on the plane of the Galaxy?" It was a private question; he spoke impulsively from interest and excitement.

The radio decoder grinned, the lines of strain vanishing from his face for a moment. "Maybe we're intercepting everybody's telephone calls, and the whole Galaxy is swarming with races that spend all day yacking at each other over the radio. Maybe the human type is standard model."

"It would take something like that," the *Times* agreed. They smiled at each other.

The *News* asked, "How did you happen to pick up television instead of voices?"

"Not by accident," Nathen explained patiently. "I'd recognized a scanning pattern, and I wanted pictures. Pictures are understandable in any language."

*

Near the interviewers, a Senator paced back and forth, muttering his memorized speech of welcome and nervously glancing out the wide streaming windows into the gray sleeting rain.

Opposite the windows of the long room was a small raised platform flanked by the tall shapes of TV cameras and sound pickups on booms, and darkened floodlights, arranged and ready for the Senator to make his speech of welcome to the aliens and the world. A shabby radio sending set stood beside it without a case to conceal its parts, two cathode television tubes flickering nakedly on one side and the speaker humming on the other. A vertical panel of dials and knobs jutted up before them and a small hand-mike sat ready on the table before the panel. It was connected to a boxlike, expensively cased piece of equipment with "Radio Lab, U.S. Property" stenciled on it.

"I recorded a couple of package screeches from Sagittarius and began working on them," Nathen added. "It took a couple of months to find the synchronizing signals and set the scanners close enough to the right time to even get a pattern. When I showed the pattern to the Department, they gave me full time to work on it, and an assistant to help. It took eight months to pick out the color bands, and assign them the right colors, to get anything intelligible on the screen."

*

The shabby-looking mess of exposed parts was the original receiver that they had labored over for ten months, adjusting and readjusting to reduce the maddening rippling plaids of unsynchronized color scanners to some kind of sane picture.

"Trial and error," said Nathen, "but it came out all right. The wide band-spread of the squawks had suggested color TV from the beginning."

He walked over and touched the set. The speaker bipped slightly and the gray screen flickered with a flash of color at the touch. The set was awake and sensitive, tuned to receive from the great interstellar spaceship which now circled the atmosphere.

"We wondered why there were so many bands, but when we got the set working, and started recording and playing everything that came in, we found we'd tapped something like a lending library line. It was all fiction, plays."

Between the pauses in Nathen's voice, the *Times* found himself unconsciously listening for the sound of roaring, swiftly approaching rocket jets.

The *Post* asked, "How did you contact the spaceship?"

"I scanned and recorded a film copy of *Rite of Spring*, the Disney-Stravinsky combination, and sent it back along the same line we were receiving from. Just testing. It wouldn't get there for a good number of years, if it got there at all, but I thought it would please the library to get a new record in.

"Two weeks later, when we caught and slowed a new batch of recordings, we found an answer. It was obviously meant for us. It was a flash of the Disney being played to a large audience, and then the audience sitting and waiting before a blank screen. The signal was very clear and loud. We'd intercepted a spaceship. They were asking for an encore, you see. They liked the film and wanted more...."

He smiled at them in sudden thought. "You can see them for yourself. It's all right down the hall where the linguists are working on the automatic translator."

The listening officer frowned and cleared his throat, and the thin young man turned to him quickly. "No security reason why they should not see the broadcasts, is there? Perhaps you should show them." He said to the reporters reassuringly, "It's right down the hall. You will be informed the moment the spaceship approaches."

The interview was very definitely over. The lank-haired, nervous young man turned away and seated himself at the radio set while the officer swallowed his objections and showed them dourly down the hall to a closed door.

They opened it and fumbled into a darkened room crowded with empty folding chairs, dominated by a glowing bright screen. The door closed behind them, bringing total darkness.

There was the sound of reporters fumbling their way into seats around him, but the *Times* man remained standing, aware of an enormous surprise, as if he had been asleep and wakened to find himself in the wrong country.

The bright colors of the double image seemed the only real thing in the darkened room. Even blurred as they were, he could see that the action was subtly different, the shapes subtly not right.

He was looking at aliens.

*

The impression was of two humans disguised, humans moving oddly, half-dancing, half-crippled. Carefully, afraid the images would go away, he reached up to his breast pocket, took out his polarized glasses, rotated one lens at right angles to the other and put them on.

Immediately, the two beings came into sharp focus, real and solid, and the screen became a wide, illusively near window through which he watched them.

They were conversing with each other in a gray-walled room, discussing something with restrained excitement. The large man in the green tunic closed his purple eyes for an instant at something the other said, and grimaced, making a motion with his fingers as if shoving something away from him.

Mellerdrammer.

The second, smaller, with yellowish-green eyes, stepped closer, talking more rapidly in a lower voice. The first stood very still, not trying to interrupt.

Obviously, the proposal was some advantageous treachery, and he wanted to be persuaded. The *Times* groped for a chair and sat down.

Perhaps gesture is universal; desire and aversion, a leaning forward or a leaning back, tension, relaxation. Perhaps these actors were masters. The scenes changed, a corridor, a parklike place in what he began to realize was a spaceship, a lecture room. There were others talking and working, speaking to the man in the green tunic, and never was it unclear what was happening or how they felt.

They talked a flowing language with many short vowels and shifts of pitch, and they gestured in the heat of talk, their hands moving with an odd lagging difference of motion, not slow, but somehow drifting.

He ignored the language, but after a time the difference in motion began to arouse his interest. Something in the way they walked....

With an effort he pulled his mind from the plot and forced his attention to the physical difference. Brown hair in short silky crew cuts, varied eye colors, the colors showing clearly because their irises were very large, their round eyes set very widely apart in tapering light-brown faces. Their necks and shoulders were thick in a way that would indicate unusual strength for a human, but their wrists were narrow and their fingers long and thin and delicate.

There seemed to be more than the usual number of fingers.

Since he came in, a machine had been whirring and a voice muttering beside him. He called his attention from counting their fingers and looked around. Beside him sat an alert-looking man wearing earphones, watching and listening with hawklike concentration. Beside him was a tall streamlined box. From the screen came the sound of the alien language. The man abruptly flipped a switch on the box, muttered a word into a small hand-microphone and flipped the switch back with nervous rapidity.

He reminded the *Times* man of the earphoned interpreters at the UN. The machine was probably a vocal translator and the mutterer a linguist adding to its vocabulary. Near the screen were two other linguists taking notes.

*

The *Times* remembered the Senator pacing in the observatory room, rehearsing his speech of welcome. The speech would not be just the empty pompous gesture he had expected. It would be translated mechanically and understood by the aliens.

On the other side of the glowing window that was the stereo screen, the large protagonist in the green tunic was speaking to a pilot in a gray uniform. They stood in a brightly lit canary-yellow control room in a spaceship.

The *Times* tried to pick up the thread of the plot. Already he was interested in the fate of the hero, and liked him. That was the effect of good acting, probably, for part of the art of acting is to win affection from the audience, and this actor might be the matinee idol of whole solar systems.

Controlled tension, betraying itself by a jerk of the hands, a too-quick answer to a question. The uniformed one, not suspicious, turned his back, busying himself at some task involving a map lit with glowing red points, his motions sharing the same fluid dragging grace of the others, as if they were underwater, or on a slow motion film. The other was watching a switch, a switch set into a panel, moving closer to it, talking casually—background music coming and rising in thin chords of tension.

There was a closeup of the alien's face watching the switch, and the *Times* noted that his ears were symmetrically half-circles, almost perfect with no earholes visible. The voice of the uniformed one answered, a brief word in a preoccupied deep voice. His back was still turned. The other glanced at the switch, moving closer to it, talking casually, the switch coming closer and closer stereoscopically. It was in reach, filling the screen. His hand came into view, darting out, closed over the switch—

There was a sharp clap of sound and his hand opened in a frozen shape of pain. Beyond him, as his gaze swung up, stood the figure of the uniformed officer, unmoving, a weapon rigid in his hand, in the startled position in which he had turned and fired, watching with widening eyes as the man in the green tunic swayed and fell.

The tableau held, the uniformed one drooping, looking down at his hand holding the weapon which had killed, and music began to build in from the background. Just for an instant, the room and the things within it flashed into one of those bewildering color changes which were the bane of color television, and switched to a color negative of itself, a green man standing in a violet control room, looking down at the body of a green man in a red tunic. It held for less than a second; then the color band alternator fell back into phase and the colors reversed to normal.

Another uniformed man came and took the weapon from the limp hand of the other, who began to explain dejectedly in a low voice while the music mounted and covered his words and the screen slowly went blank, like a window that slowly filmed over with gray fog.

PICTURES DON'T LIE

The music faded.

In the dark, someone clapped appreciatively.

The earphoned man beside the *Times* shifted his earphones back from his ears and spoke briskly. "I can't get any more. Either of you want a replay?"

There was a short silence until the linguist nearest the set said, "I guess we've squeezed that one dry. Let's run the tape where Nathen and that ship radio boy are kidding around CQing and tuning their beams in closer. I have a hunch the boy is talking routine ham talk and giving the old radio count—one-two-three-testing."

There was some fumbling in the semi-dark and then the screen came to life again.

*

It showed a flash of an audience sitting before a screen and gave a clipped chord of some familiar symphony. "Crazy about Stravinsky and Mozart," remarked the earphoned linguist to the *Times*, resetting his earphones. "Can't stand Gershwin. Can you beat that?" He turned his attention back to the screen as the right sequence came on.

The *Post*, who was sitting just in front of him, turned to the *Times* and said, "Funny how much they look like people." He was writing, making notes to telephone his report. "What color hair did that character have?"

"I didn't notice." He wondered if he should remind the reporter that Nathen had said he assigned the color bands on guess, choosing the colors that gave the most plausible images. The guests, when they arrived, could turn out to be bright green with blue hair. Only the gradations of color in the picture were sure, only the similarities and contrasts, the relationship of one color to another.

From the screen came the sound of the alien language again. This race averaged deeper voices than human. He liked deep voices. Could he write that?

No, there was something wrong with that, too. How had Nathen established the right sound-track pitch? Was it a matter of taking the modulation as it came in, or some sort of hetrodyning up and down by trial and error? Probably.

It might be safer to assume that Nathen had simply preferred deep voices.

As he sat there, doubting, an uneasiness he had seen in Nathen came back to add to his own uncertainty, and he remembered just how close that uneasiness had come to something that looked like restrained fear.

"What I don't get is why he went to all the trouble of picking up TV shows instead of just contacting them," the *News* complained. "They're good shows, but what's the point?"

"Maybe so we'd get to learn their language too," said the *Herald*.

On the screen now was the obviously unstaged and genuine scene of a young alien working over a bank of apparatus. He turned and waved and opened his mouth in the comical O shape which the *Times* was beginning to recognize as their equivalent of a smile, then went back to trying to explain something about the equipment, in elaborate awkward gestures and carefully mouthed words.

The *Times* got up quietly, went out into the bright white stone corridor and walked back the way he had come, thoughtfully folding his stereo glasses and putting them away.

No one stopped him. Secrecy restrictions were ambiguous here. The reticence of the Army seemed more a matter of habit, mere reflex, from the fact that it had all originated in the Intelligence Department, than any reasoned policy of keeping the landing a secret.

The main room was more crowded than he had left it. The TV camera and sound crew stood near their apparatus, the Senator had found a chair and was reading, and at the far end of the room eight men were grouped in a circle of chairs, arguing something with impassioned concentration. The *Times* recognized a few he knew personally, eminent names in science, workers in field theory.

A stray phrase reached him: "—reference to the universal constants as ratio—" It was probably a discussion of ways of converting formulas from one mathematics to another for a rapid exchange of information.

They had reason to be intent, aware of the flood of insights that novel viewpoints could bring, if they could grasp them. He would have liked to go over and listen, but there was too little time left before the spaceship was due, and he had a question to ask.

*

The hand-rigged transceiver was still humming, tuned to the sending band of the circling ship, and the young man who had started it all was sitting on the edge of the TV platform with his chin resting in one hand. He did not look up as the *Times* approached, but it was the indifference of preoccupation, not discourtesy.

The *Times* sat down on the edge of the platform beside him and took out a pack of cigarettes, then remembered the coming TV broadcast and the ban on smoking. He put them away, thoughtfully watching the diminishing rain spray against the streaming windows.

"What's wrong?" he asked.

Nathen showed that he was aware and friendly by a slight motion of his head.

"*You* tell me."

"Hunch," said the *Times* man. "Sheer hunch. Everything sailing along too smoothly, everyone taking too much for granted."

Nathen relaxed slightly. "I'm still listening."

"Something about the way they move...."

Nathen shifted to glance at him.

"That's bothered me, too."

"Are you sure they're adjusted to the right speed?"

Nathen clenched his hands out in front of him and looked at them consideringly. "I don't know. When I turn the tape faster, they're all rushing, and you begin to wonder why their clothes don't stream behind them, why the doors close so quickly and yet you can't hear them slam, why things fall so fast. If I turn it slower, they all seem to be swimming." He gave the *Times* a considering sidewise glance. "Didn't catch the name."

Country-bred guy, thought the *Times*. "Jacob Luke, *Times*," he said, extending his hand.

Nathen gave the hand a quick, hard grip, identifying the name. "Sunday Science Section editor. I read it. Surprised to meet you here."

"Likewise." The *Times* smiled. "Look, have you gone into this rationally, with formulas?" He found a pencil in his pocket. "Obviously there's something wrong with our judgment of their weight-to-speed-to-momentum ratio. Maybe it's something simple like low gravity aboard ship, with magnetic shoes. Maybe they *are* floating slightly."

"Why worry?" Nathen cut in. "I don't see any reason to try to figure it out now." He laughed and shoved back his black hair nervously. "We'll see them in twenty minutes."

"Will we?" asked the *Times* slowly.

There was a silence while the Senator turned a page of his magazine with a slight crackling of paper, and the scientists argued at the other end of the room. Nathen pushed at his lank black hair again, as if it were trying to fall forward in front of his eyes and keep him from seeing.

"Sure." The young man laughed suddenly, talked rapidly. "Sure we'll see them. Why shouldn't we, with all the government ready with welcome speeches, the whole Army turned out and hiding over the hill, reporters all around, newsreel cameras—everything set up to broadcast the landing to the world. The President himself shaking hands with me and waiting in Washington—"

He came to the truth without pausing for breath.

PICTURES DON'T LIE

He said, "Hell, no, they won't get here. There's some mistake somewhere. Something's wrong. I should have told the brasshats yesterday when I started adding it up. Don't know why I didn't say anything. Scared, I guess. Too much top rank around here. Lost my nerve."

He clutched the *Times* man's sleeve. "Look. I don't know what—"

A green light flashed on the sending-receiving set. Nathen didn't look at it, but he stopped talking.

*

The loudspeaker on the set broke into a voice speaking in the alien's language. The Senator started and looked nervously at it, straightening his tie. The voice stopped.

Nathen turned and looked at the loudspeaker. His worry seemed to be gone.

"What is it?" the *Times* asked anxiously.

"He says they've slowed enough to enter the atmosphere now. They'll be here in five to ten minutes, I guess. That's Bud. He's all excited. He says holy smoke, what a murky-looking planet we live on." Nathen smiled. "Kidding."

The *Times* was puzzled. "What does he mean, murky? It can't be raining over much territory on Earth." Outside, the rain was slowing and bright blue patches of sky were shining through breaks in the cloud blanket, glittering blue light from the drops that ran down the windows. He tried to think of an explanation. "Maybe they're trying to land on Venus." The thought was ridiculous, he knew. The spaceship was following Nathen's sending beam. It couldn't miss Earth. "Bud" had to be kidding.

The green light glowed on the set again, and they stopped speaking, waiting for the message to be recorded, slowed and replayed. The cathode screen came to life suddenly with a picture of the young man sitting at his sending-set, his back turned, watching a screen at one side which showed a glimpse of a huge dark plain approaching. As the ship plunged down toward it, the illusion of solidity melted into

18

a boiling turbulence of black clouds. They expanded in an inky swirl, looked huge for an instant, and then blackness swallowed the screen. The young alien swung around to face the camera, speaking a few words as he moved, made the O of a smile again, then flipped the switch and the screen went gray.

Nathen's voice was suddenly toneless and strained. "He said something like break out the drinks, here they come."

"The atmosphere doesn't look like that," the *Times* said at random, knowing he was saying something too obvious even to think about. "Not Earth's atmosphere."

Some people drifted up. "What did they say?"

"Entering the atmosphere, ought to be landing in five or ten minutes," Nathen told them.

A ripple of heightened excitement ran through the room. Cameramen began adjusting the lens angles again, turning on the mike and checking it, turning on the floodlights. The scientists rose and stood near the window, still talking. The reporters trooped in from the hall and went to the windows to watch for the great event. The three linguists came in, trundling a large wheeled box that was the mechanical translator, supervising while it was hitched into the sound broadcasting system.

"Landing where?" the *Times* asked Nathen brutally. "Why don't you do something?"

"Tell me what to do and I'll do it," Nathen said quietly, not moving.

It was not sarcasm. Jacob Luke of the *Times* looked sidewise at the strained whiteness of his face, and moderated his tone. "Can't you contact them?"

"Not while they're landing."

"What now?" The *Times* took out a pack of cigarettes, remembered the rule against smoking, and put it back.

"We just wait." Nathen leaned his elbow on one knee and his chin in his hand.

PICTURES DON'T LIE

They waited.

*

All the people in the room were waiting. There was no more conversation. A bald man of the scientist group was automatically buffing his fingernails over and over and inspecting them without seeing them, another absently polished his glasses, held them up to the light, put them on, and then a moment later took them off and began polishing again. The television crew concentrated on their jobs, moving quietly and efficiently, with perfectionist care, minutely arranging things which did not need to be arranged, checking things that had already been checked.

This was to be one of the great moments of human history, and they were all trying to forget that fact and remain impassive and wrapped up in the problems of their jobs as good specialists should.

After an interminable age the *Times* consulted his watch. Three minutes had passed. He tried holding his breath a moment, listening for a distant approaching thunder of jets. There was no sound.

The sun came out from behind the clouds and lit up the field like a great spotlight on an empty stage.

Abruptly the green light shone on the set again, indicating that a squawk message had been received. The recorder recorded it, slowed it and fed it back to the speaker. It clicked and the sound was very loud in the still, tense room.

The screen remained gray, but Bud's voice spoke a few words in the alien language. He stopped, the speaker clicked and the light went out. When it was plain that nothing more would occur and no announcement was to be made of what was said, the people in the room turned back to the windows, talk picked up again.

Somebody told a joke and laughed alone.

One of the linguists remained turned toward the loudspeaker, then looked at the widening patches of blue sky showing out the window, his expression puzzled. He had understood.

"It's dark," the thin Intelligence Department decoder translated, low-voiced, to the man from the *Times*. "Your atmosphere is *thick*. That's precisely what Bud said."

Another three minutes. The *Times* caught himself about to light a cigarette and swore silently, blowing the match out and putting the cigarette back into its package. He listened for the sound of the rocket jets. It was time for the landing, yet he heard no blasts.

The green light came on in the transceiver.

Message in.

Instinctively he came to his feet. Nathen abruptly was standing beside him. Then the message came in the voice he was coming to think of as Bud. It spoke and paused. Suddenly the *Times* knew.

"We've landed." Nathen whispered the words.

The wind blew across the open spaces of white concrete and damp soil that was the empty airfield, swaying the wet, shiny grass. The people in the room looked out, listening for the roar of jets, looking for the silver bulk of a spaceship in the sky.

Nathen moved, seating himself at the transmitter, switching it on to warm up, checking and balancing dials. Jacob Luke of the *Times* moved softly to stand behind his right shoulder, hoping he could be useful. Nathen made a half motion of his head, as if to glance back at him, unhooked two of the earphone sets hanging on the side of the tall streamlined box that was the automatic translator, plugged them in and handed one back over his shoulder to the *Times* man.

The voice began to come from the speaker again.

Hastily, Jacob Luke fitted the earphones over his ears. He fancied he could hear Bud's voice tremble. For a moment it was just Bud's voice speaking the alien language, and then, very distant and clear in his earphones, he heard the recorded voice of the linguist say an English word, then a mechanical click and another clear word in the voice of one of the other translators, then another as the alien's voice flowed from the loudspeaker, the cool single words barely audible, overlapping and blending with it like translating thought, skipping unfamiliar words, yet quite astonishingly clear.

"Radar shows no buildings or civilization near. The atmosphere around us registers as thick as glue. Tremendous gas pressure, low gravity, no light at all. You didn't describe it like this. Where are you, Joe? This isn't some kind of trick, is it?" Bud hesitated, was prompted by a deeper official voice and jerked out the words.

"If it is a trick, we are ready to repel attack."

*

The linguist stood listening. He whitened slowly and beckoned the other linguists over to him and whispered to them.

Joseph Nathen looked at them with unwarranted bitter hostility while he picked up the hand-mike, plugging it into the translator. "Joe calling," he said quietly into it in clear, slow English. "No trick. We don't know where you are. I am trying to get a direction fix from your signal. Describe your surroundings to us if at all possible."

Nearby, the floodlights blazed steadily on the television platform, ready for the official welcome of the aliens to Earth. The television channels of the world had been alerted to set aside their scheduled programs for an unscheduled great event. In the long room the people waited, listening for the swelling sound of rocket jets.

This time, after the light came on, there was a long delay. The speaker sputtered, and sputtered again, building to a steady scratching they could barely sense as a dim voice. It came through in a few tinny words and then wavered back to inaudibility. The machine translated in their earphones.

"Tried ... seemed ... repair...." Suddenly it came in clearly. "Can't tell if the auxiliary blew, too. Will try it. We might pick you up clearly on the next try. I have the volume down. Where is the landing port? Repeat. Where is the landing port? Where are you?"

Nathen put down the hand-mike and carefully set a dial on the recording box, and flipped a switch, speaking over his shoulder. "This sets it to repeat what I said the last time. It keeps repeating." Then he sat with unnatural stillness, his head still half turned, as if he had suddenly caught a glimpse of answer and was trying with no success whatever to grasp it.

The green warning light cut in, the recording clicked and the playback of Bud's face and voice appeared on the screen.

"We heard a few words, Joe, and then the receiver blew again. We're adjusting a viewing screen to pick up the long waves that go through the murk and convert them to visible light. We'll be able to see out soon. The engineer says that something is wrong with the stern jets, and the captain has had me broadcast a help call to our nearest space base." He made the mouth O of a grin. "The message won't reach it for some years. I trust you, Joe, but get us out of here, will you?—They're buzzing that the screen is finally ready. Hold everything."

*

The screen went gray, and the green light went off.

The *Times* considered the lag required for the help call, the speaking and recording of the message just received, the time needed to reconvert a viewing screen.

"They work fast." He shifted uneasily, and added at random, "Something wrong with the time factor. All wrong. They work *too* fast."

The green light came on again immediately. Nathen half turned to him, sliding his words hastily into the gap of time as the message was recorded and slowed. "They're close enough for our transmission power to blow their receiver."

If it was on Earth, why the darkness around the ship? "Maybe they see in the high ultra-violet—the atmosphere is opaque to that band," the *Times* suggested hastily as the speaker began to talk in the young extraterrestrial's voice.

It *was* shaking now. "Stand by for the description."

They tensed, waiting. The *Times* brought a map of the state before his mind's eye.

23

PICTURES DON'T LIE

"A half circle of cliffs around the horizon. A wide muddy lake swarming with swimming things. Huge, strange white foliage all around the ship and incredibly huge pulpy monsters attacking and eating each other on all sides. We almost landed in the lake, right on the soft edge. The mud can't hold the ship's weight, and we're sinking. The engineer says we might be able to blast free, but the tubes are mud-clogged and might blow up the ship. When can you reach us?"

The *Times* thought vaguely of the Carboniferous Era. Nathen obviously had seen something he had not.

"Where are they?" the *Times* asked him quietly.

Nathen pointed to the antenna position indicators. The *Times* let his eyes follow the converging imaginary lines of focus out the window to the sunlit airfield, the empty airfield, the drying concrete and green waving grass where the lines met.

Where the lines met. The spaceship was there!

The fear of something unknown gripped him suddenly.

The spaceship was broadcasting again. "*Where are you? Answer if possible! We are sinking! Where are you?*"

He saw that Nathen knew. "What is it?" the *Times* asked hoarsely. "Are they in another dimension or the past or on another world or what?"

Nathen was smiling bitterly, and Jacob Luke remembered that the young man had a friend in that spaceship. "My guess is that they evolved on a high-gravity planet, with a thin atmosphere, near a blue-white star. Sure they see in the ultra-violet range. Our sun is abnormally small and dim and yellow. Our atmosphere is so thick, it screens out ultra-violet." He laughed harshly. "A good joke on us, the weird place we evolved in, the thing it did to us!"

"Where are you?" called the alien spaceship. "Hurry, please! We're sinking!"

*

24

The decoder slowed his tumbled, frightened words and looked up into the *Times'* face for understanding. "We'll rescue them," he said quietly. "You were right about the time factor, right about them moving at a different speed. I misunderstood. This business about squawk coding, speeding for better transmission to counteract beam waver—I was wrong."

"What do you mean?"

"They don't speed up their broadcasts."

"They don't—?"

Suddenly, in his mind's eye, the *Times* began to see again the play he had just seen—but the actors were moving at blurring speed, the words jerking out in a fluting, dizzying stream, thoughts and decisions passing with unfollowable rapidity, rippling faces in a twisting blur of expressions, doors slamming wildly, shatteringly, as the actors leaped in and out of rooms.

No—faster, faster—he wasn't visualizing it as rapidly as it was, an hour of talk and action in one almost instantaneous "squawk," a narrow peak of "noise" interfering with a single word in an Earth broadcast! Faster—faster—it was impossible. Matter could not stand such stress—inertia—momentum—abrupt weight.

It was insane. "Why?" he asked. "How?"

Nathen laughed again harshly, reaching for the mike. "Get them out? There isn't a lake or river within hundreds of miles from here!"

A shiver of unreality went down the *Times'* spine. Automatically and inanely, he found himself delving in his pocket for a cigarette while he tried to grasp what had happened. "Where are they, then? Why can't we see their spaceship?"

Nathen switched the microphone on in a gesture that showed the bitterness of his disappointment.

"We'll need a magnifying glass for that."

www.ingramcontent.com/pod-product-compliance
Lightning Source LLC
Chambersburg PA
CBHW021006150626

46549CB00012BA/1381